CHILDREN'S STORYTIME TREASURY

Grimm's Fairytales

A PARRAGON BOOK

PUBLISHED BY PARRAGON BOOK SERVICE LTD.
UNITS 13-17, AVONBRIDGE TRADING ESTATE, ATLANTIC ROAD,
AVONMOUTH, BRISTOL BS11 9QD

PRODUCED BY THE TEMPLAR COMPANY PLC,
PIPPBROOK MILL, LONDON ROAD, DORKING, SURREY RH4 1JE

COPYRIGHT © 1996 PARRAGON BOOK SERVICE LIMITED

DESIGNED BY MARK KINGSLEY-MONKS

PRINTED AND BOUND IN SPAIN

ISBN 0-75252-036-9

CHILDREN'S STORYTIME TREASURY

Grimm's Fairytales

• PARRAGON •

The Frog Prince
Illustrated by John James

Once upon a time there lived a King and Queen. They had three beautiful daughters but the youngest Princess was so lovely that she gladdened the heart of everyone who saw her. She was a merry child and her favourite toy was a golden ball which sparkled in the sunshine.

One summer's day the sun shone from a cloudless blue sky and there was not a breath of wind to stir the air. It was so hot that the little Princess decided to play in the shade of the wood. Slowly she walked amongst the tall trees and their long shadows were cool and soothing after the glaring heat of the sun.

Soon she could hear the sound of splashing water and, following the sound, she came upon an open glade where a fountain tumbled into a silvery pool. What a lovely sight! With a cry of delight, the Princess threw her ball high into the air and ran to catch it — but to her dismay the ball slipped through her fingers, rolled over the ground and fell into the pool.

With a cry of alarm she knelt by the pool and tried to reach it but the ball quickly sank from sight. How she wept at the loss of her precious toy.

Her tears fell into the pool and ripples spread over the still, grey water. Suddenly she heard a little voice.

"Princess, why do you weep so sadly?" it said, and to her surprise, there sat a green frog on a large lily pad.

The Princess sighed deeply. "I have lost my golden ball," she explained, wiping a tear from her cheek. "I fear it is gone forever." The Frog spoke again.

"If I find your ball for you, you must promise me something in return," he said solemnly.

"I will promise you anything!" cried the Princess.

"You must promise me that I can eat from your own golden plate and sleep in your own golden bed, and then I will fetch your golden ball," said the Frog.

The Princess did not like the sound of this at all!

"I will pretend to agree to what he says," she decided, "but as soon as I have my ball I will run home and he will never be able to find me." And so that is just what she did and the poor Frog was left alone on his lily pad.

That evening as the Princess sat down to eat she had forgotten all about the Frog in the pond. But the Frog had not forgotten her. He had found his way to the palace and at that moment was sitting outside the door.

Suddenly the Princess heard a small voice.

"Open the door, my Princess dear.
Open the door to your true love here!
And remember the words that you and I said
By the fountain cool in the greenwood shade."
"Who is that, my daughter?" asked her father, the
King. Then the unhappy Princess explained all that had
happened in the wood and her father looked grave.
  "You must honour your promise," he said. "The Frog
kept his word and now you must keep yours."

The Princess opened the door with a heavy heart and there sat the Frog. Slowly she returned to her seat and the Frog followed, *flip, flop, flip, flop.* The Queen, the Princess's two elder sisters and all the Ladies-in-Waiting shuddered with horror as the warty little creature passed by, and when he hopped upon the table they moaned and hid their faces in their napkins.

The Princess wrinkled her beautiful nose in disgust as the Frog crept close to her plate and with a long darting tongue ate up her peas one by one. At last he sat back and yawned.

"Now I am sleepy," he said. "Please take me to your room for I wish to sleep upon your pillow."

The Princess was horrified. She looked imploringly at her father but the King shook his head.

"It may seem hard, little daughter," he said, "but you must do as he asks. A promise is a promise." So she carried the Frog upstairs and soon he lay fast asleep upon her silken pillow. The Princess vowed she would not sleep a wink all night but after a while her eyelids drooped and soon she, too, slept. The next morning when she awoke the Frog was nowhere to be seen.

"At last I am rid of the horrid creature," thought the Princess to herself— but she spoke too soon! That evening as she sat down to eat her meal the same little voice could be heard outside the door.

"Open the door, my Princess dear.
Open the door to your true love here!
And remember the words that you and I said
By the fountain cool in the greenwood shade."
There sat the Frog once again, and once again he
asked to eat from her plate and once again the Princess
had to do as he wished. There he sat upon the linen
tablecloth and the Ladies-in Waiting shrieked in disgust
as the little creature happily licked the cherries on top
of the iced cakes.

When he had eaten his fill he asked to be taken to the Princess's golden bed and there he slept as before upon her silken pillow. The little Princess had no choice but to sleep by his side and after much shedding of tears she fell fast asleep beside him.

The next morning the sunbeams crept through her bedroom window and as they touched her soft cheek, the Princess awoke. She opened her eyes slowly, dreading the sight of the Frog beside her on her pillow. But he was nowhere in sight.

Instead she found herself gazing into the eyes of the
most handsome Prince she had ever seen.

"Sweet Princess, please accept my deepest thanks," he
said as he took her hand. "You have saved me from a
wicked spell. An evil witch turned me into a Frog and
banished me forever to the fountain pool. The only
person who could break the spell was a Princess who
would let me eat from her plate and sleep on her
pillow." The Prince stroked her hair gently.

"You did this for me, ugly as I was, and now the spell is broken and I am free." He knelt upon one knee.

"Please marry me and share my happiness forever," he begged. The Princess agreed at once and so they were married and when the wedding was over a white coach pulled by eight white horses pulled up outside the palace. It was driven by Faithful Henry, the Prince's servant, and as the happy man jingled the reins, the joyful couple drove off to begin their new life together.

Hansel and Grettel
Illustrated by Annabel Spenceley

Once upon a time long ago there lived a poor woodcutter and his two children, Hansel and Grettel. The children's mother had died when they were very young and their father had married again. Their stepmother was a wicked woman and she did not love Hansel and Grettel. The woodcutter had very little money to spend on food and so all four of them went hungry for much of the week.

Late one night as the two children lay shivering in their beds they heard their stepmother talking.

"Something must be done or we will all starve to death," the woman whispered to the children's father. "We have enough food for two mouths, but not for four. We must get rid of Hansel and Grettel."

Grettel wept bitterly as she heard her stepmother describe how she would lead the children deep into the forest and leave them there to perish.

"I will find a way home, little sister," said Hansel.

The next morning the children were taken far away.

"Stay here until we return," said their stepmother. Soon night fell and they were left quite alone.

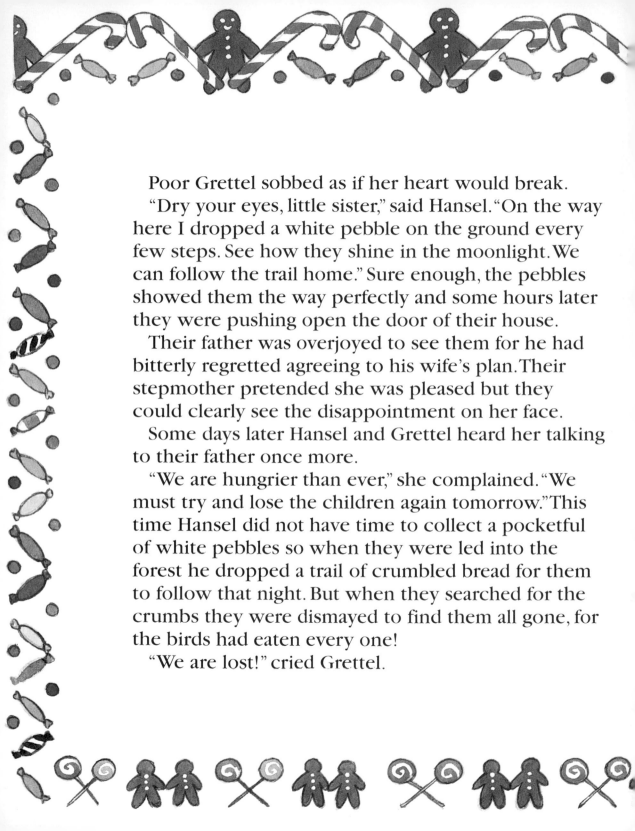

Poor Grettel sobbed as if her heart would break.

"Dry your eyes, little sister," said Hansel. "On the way here I dropped a white pebble on the ground every few steps. See how they shine in the moonlight. We can follow the trail home." Sure enough, the pebbles showed them the way perfectly and some hours later they were pushing open the door of their house.

Their father was overjoyed to see them for he had bitterly regretted agreeing to his wife's plan. Their stepmother pretended she was pleased but they could clearly see the disappointment on her face.

Some days later Hansel and Grettel heard her talking to their father once more.

"We are hungrier than ever," she complained. "We must try and lose the children again tomorrow." This time Hansel did not have time to collect a pocketful of white pebbles so when they were led into the forest he dropped a trail of crumbled bread for them to follow that night. But when they searched for the crumbs they were dismayed to find them all gone, for the birds had eaten every one!

"We are lost!" cried Grettel.

Again and again they tried to find a way out of the forest but every path they took led them ever deeper into the wood. Suddenly Hansel saw a white dove sitting upon a branch. She twittered at them, then flew off over the trees.

"I believe she is telling us to follow her," said Hansel and with weary steps they trudged after the little bird. She sang as if to encourage them on their way and after a time they found themselves in an open glade. And there in the middle of the clearing was the most perfect little gingerbread cottage.

"Oh, Hansel!" gasped Grettel. "The roof is made of honey cake and the windows are made of barley sugar! I must just nibble a little corner." Soon they were both munching away on their favourite bits of the house and nothing had ever tasted quite so delicious.

All of a sudden the door flew open and out hobbled an old dame leaning upon a stick. The children drew back in fear but the old lady smiled at them kindly.

"Welcome to my home, my dears," she said. "Come inside and I will look after you." She fed them sweet pancakes, then put them to bed under cosy quilts.

But when Hansel and Grettel awoke next day the old lady's kind manner had changed. Her weak eyes glinted cruelly as she grabbed Hansel by the arm.

"You will make a tasty morsel for me to eat," she cackled and then the children saw that they had been tricked. The old lady was a witch and she meant to make a meal of them! Laughing cruelly, she bundled Hansel into a cage.

"I will fatten you up before I cook you," she hissed and Hansel shook with fear. Every day she checked to see how fat he was getting but clever Hansel stuck an old bone through the bars and when the old crone pinched it, she decided he was still too thin to eat.

At last the witch could wait no longer.

"Fat or thin, I will eat him as he is," she decided, clutching at Grettel with one claw-like hand. "And you will help me prepare the cooking pot."

How the little girl sobbed as she carried the water and lit the fire under the oven. The witch scowled at her and stamped her feet.

"Stop your wailing," she shouted. "Just climb in the oven and tell me how hot it is." Then Grettel had a clever idea. She looked up at the Witch timidly.

"I don't know how to climb inside the oven," she said anxiously. "Can you show me?"

The witch stamped her foot again, but moved close to the oven entrance.

"Why, you silly goose," she said crossly, "it is perfectly simple. All you have to do is put one foot here and then you can step right inside." But as the witch showed her where to put her feet Grettel suddenly ran at her and with a great shove pushed the old hag right inside the oven and slammed the iron door tight shut. Gracious, how the old witch yelled! Soon Hansel was free from the cage and jumping for joy.

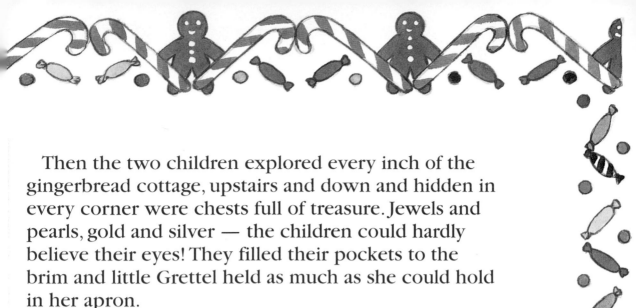

Then the two children explored every inch of the gingerbread cottage, upstairs and down and hidden in every corner were chests full of treasure. Jewels and pearls, gold and silver — the children could hardly believe their eyes! They filled their pockets to the brim and little Grettel held as much as she could hold in her apron.

Soon they were ready and they set off to find their way home. After a while they came to a large lake but they could find no way of crossing the water.

"Now we will never see Father again," sighed Hansel, but just then a large white duck came swimming by.

"I will carry you over on my back," she offered and so the two grateful children were delivered safe to the other side. For many hours they walked under the shade of the trees and after a time the forest began to look more familiar and then, to their delight, Hansel and Grettel saw their own little home in front of them.

Their father wept for joy as he gathered the children into his arms for he had not had a single happy hour since he had lost them.

"Your wicked stepmother has gone away for good," he said. "Now we will be together forever."

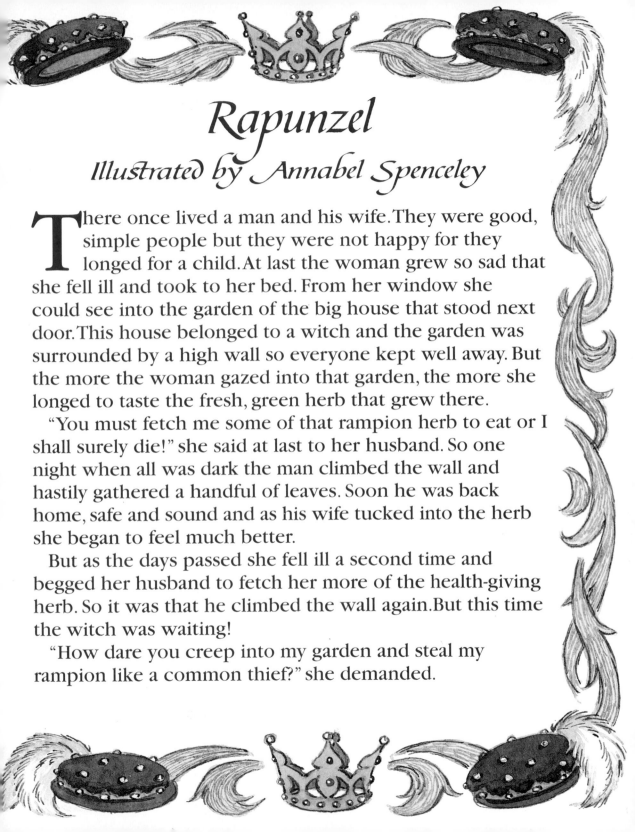

Rapunzel

Illustrated by Annabel Spenceley

There once lived a man and his wife. They were good, simple people but they were not happy for they longed for a child. At last the woman grew so sad that she fell ill and took to her bed. From her window she could see into the garden of the big house that stood next door. This house belonged to a witch and the garden was surrounded by a high wall so everyone kept well away. But the more the woman gazed into that garden, the more she longed to taste the fresh, green herb that grew there.

"You must fetch me some of that rampion herb to eat or I shall surely die!" she said at last to her husband. So one night when all was dark the man climbed the wall and hastily gathered a handful of leaves. Soon he was back home, safe and sound and as his wife tucked into the herb she began to feel much better.

But as the days passed she fell ill a second time and begged her husband to fetch her more of the health-giving herb. So it was that he climbed the wall again. But this time the witch was waiting!

"How dare you creep into my garden and steal my rampion like a common thief?" she demanded.

The poor man fell to his knees, covered his eyes and quivered like a leaf.

"Forgive me!" he begged. "My wife could see the plant from her window and it looked so good that she longed to taste it." This compliment softened the witch a little, but then her eyes grew cunning.

"I shall let you go free on one condition," she hissed. "Your wife will soon have a baby but when it is a week old you must give it to me." The man was so terrified that he would have agreed to anything.

"Yes, yes," he gasped and without a backward look he scrambled over the wall and ran for home.

Some months after this, his wife did indeed have a baby daughter and great was their joy. But on the seventh day after her birth the witch swept into the room, plucked the child from the cradle and was gone! The man and his wife were grief-stricken but however hard they searched, they never saw the witch or their daughter again.

The witch raised the little girl all alone and named her Rapunzel, for that is another name for the rampion plant. When Rapunzel was sixteen the witch locked her away in a tall tower in the middle of the forest and each day she would visit her and call out:

"Rapunzel, Rapunzel, let down your golden hair!"

Then Rapunzel would let her long plaits fall from the window and the witch would hold on and climb up hand over hand.

So the time passed and poor lonely Rapunzel would sing to herself to while away the hours. Her voice was like sweet birdsong and one day it was heard by a Prince who was riding by. He hid behind a tree when the witch arrived and watched as she clambered up into the tower. He longed to meet the girl with the lovely voice and so when the witch had gone, he climbed up Rapunzel's plaits and jumped inside the room.

Rapunzel was astonished to see this handsome stranger kneeling before her but he spoke to her gently.

"Have no fear," he said. "You have won my heart with your beautiful singing and now my happiness would be complete if you would agree to become my bride."

Rapunzel did not need to think twice and soon they they had planned her escape.

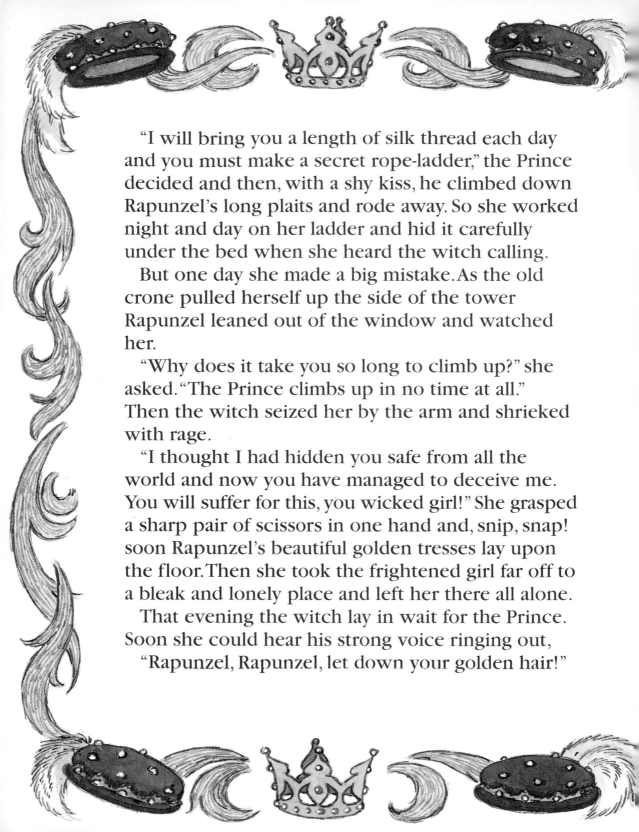

"I will bring you a length of silk thread each day and you must make a secret rope-ladder," the Prince decided and then, with a shy kiss, he climbed down Rapunzel's long plaits and rode away. So she worked night and day on her ladder and hid it carefully under the bed when she heard the witch calling.

But one day she made a big mistake. As the old crone pulled herself up the side of the tower Rapunzel leaned out of the window and watched her.

"Why does it take you so long to climb up?" she asked. "The Prince climbs up in no time at all." Then the witch seized her by the arm and shrieked with rage.

"I thought I had hidden you safe from all the world and now you have managed to deceive me. You will suffer for this, you wicked girl!" She grasped a sharp pair of scissors in one hand and, snip, snap! soon Rapunzel's beautiful golden tresses lay upon the floor. Then she took the frightened girl far off to a bleak and lonely place and left her there all alone.

That evening the witch lay in wait for the Prince. Soon she could hear his strong voice ringing out,

"Rapunzel, Rapunzel, let down your golden hair!"

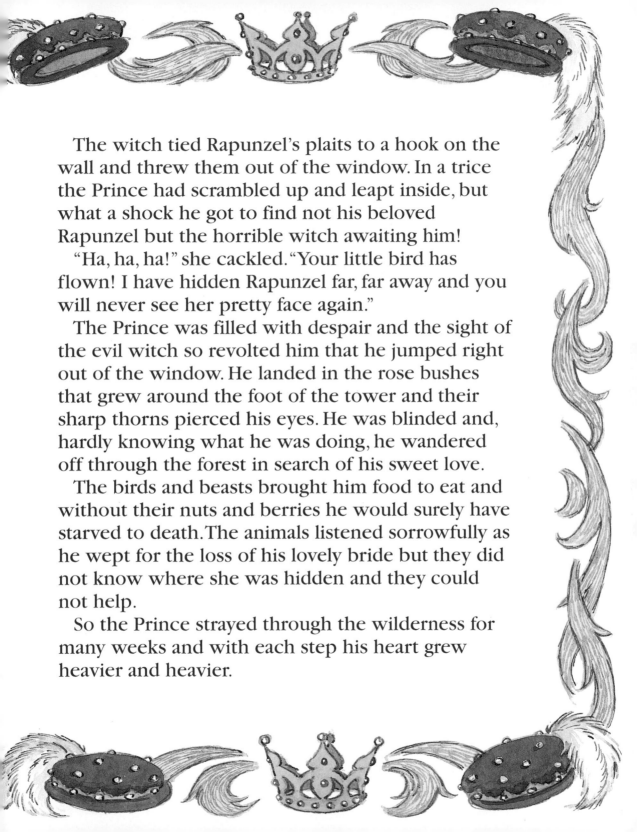

The witch tied Rapunzel's plaits to a hook on the wall and threw them out of the window. In a trice the Prince had scrambled up and leapt inside, but what a shock he got to find not his beloved Rapunzel but the horrible witch awaiting him!

"Ha, ha, ha!" she cackled. "Your little bird has flown! I have hidden Rapunzel far, far away and you will never see her pretty face again."

The Prince was filled with despair and the sight of the evil witch so revolted him that he jumped right out of the window. He landed in the rose bushes that grew around the foot of the tower and their sharp thorns pierced his eyes. He was blinded and, hardly knowing what he was doing, he wandered off through the forest in search of his sweet love.

The birds and beasts brought him food to eat and without their nuts and berries he would surely have starved to death. The animals listened sorrowfully as he wept for the loss of his lovely bride but they did not know where she was hidden and they could not help.

So the Prince strayed through the wilderness for many weeks and with each step his heart grew heavier and heavier.

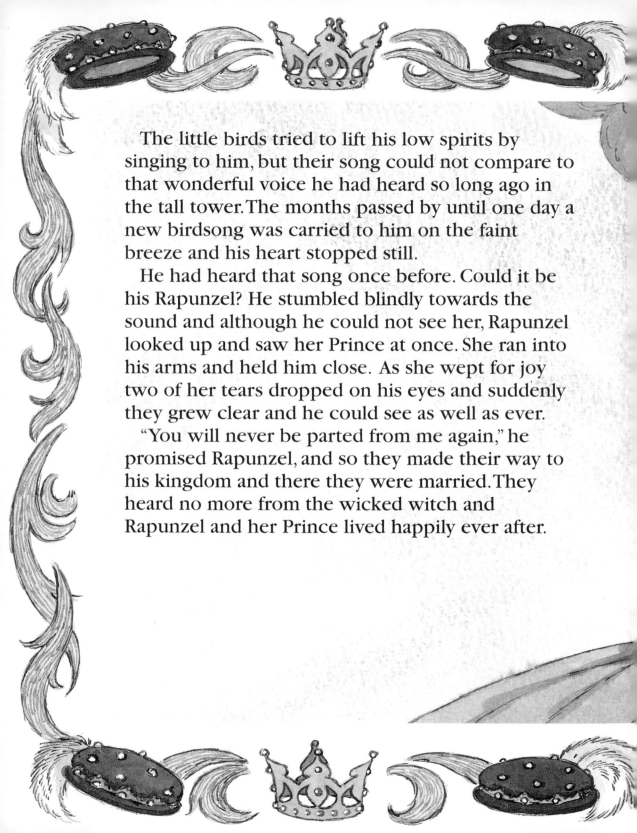

The little birds tried to lift his low spirits by singing to him, but their song could not compare to that wonderful voice he had heard so long ago in the tall tower. The months passed by until one day a new birdsong was carried to him on the faint breeze and his heart stopped still.

He had heard that song once before. Could it be his Rapunzel? He stumbled blindly towards the sound and although he could not see her, Rapunzel looked up and saw her Prince at once. She ran into his arms and held him close. As she wept for joy two of her tears dropped on his eyes and suddenly they grew clear and he could see as well as ever.

"You will never be parted from me again," he promised Rapunzel, and so they made their way to his kingdom and there they were married. They heard no more from the wicked witch and Rapunzel and her Prince lived happily ever after.

The Golden Goose
Illustrated by Claire Mumford

Once upon a time there were three brothers. The youngest son was given the name of Dummling and was laughed at by his family and everyone else.

One day the eldest son went into the forest to cut some wood. His mother gave him cake and a bottle of wine and off he went, whistling cheerfully. But he had no sooner set to work than a little old man appeared.

"I am so hungry and thirsty. May I have some cake and wine?" he asked. But the eldest son shook his head.

"Be off with you," he said gruffly. "I will share my meal with no-one." But it seemed the old man was going to get his revenge with the very next swing of the axe for it landed on the eldest son's foot. How he yelled! The next day the second son decided to try his luck and once again his mother gave him cake and wine.

The little old man approached the second son and asked to share his meal, but the second son also refused. He, too, was cut by the next swing of the axe.

The next day Dummling set off for the forest to cut some wood. He was given only bread and water but was happy to share what he had with the little man.

"You are a good boy," said the man, "and if you cut down that tree you will get your reward." Dummling did as he was bid and was astonished to find a goose covered entirely with golden feathers.

"I will go to the city and seek my fortune," Dummling decided. "This beautiful goose will bring me luck." As he strolled along the lane he passed a girl. She gasped to see such a glorious golden bird and stretched out her hand to stroke it. But imagine her dismay when she found that she could not take her hand away! The goose had magic powers and whoever laid a finger on her soon found themselves stuck fast to her feathers.

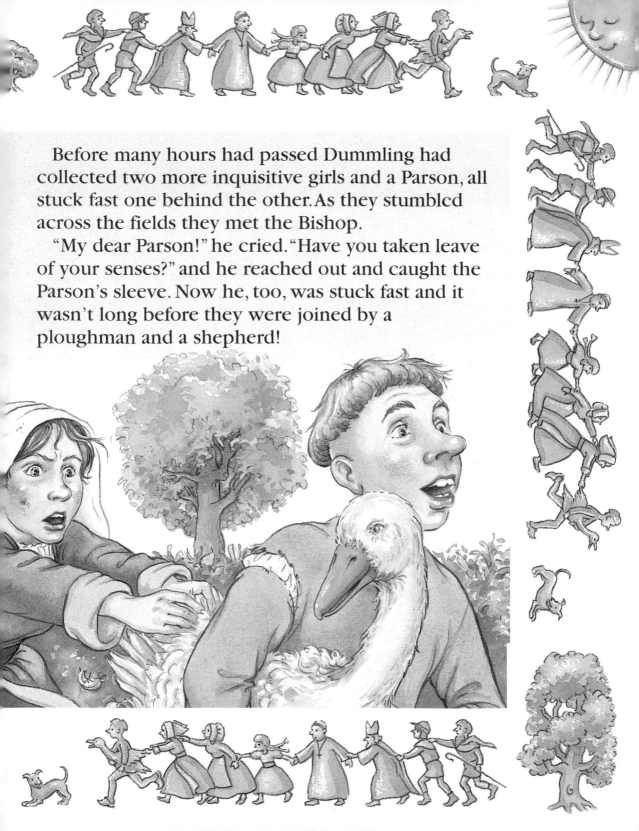

Before many hours had passed Dummling had collected two more inquisitive girls and a Parson, all stuck fast one behind the other. As they stumbled across the fields they met the Bishop.

"My dear Parson!" he cried. "Have you taken leave of your senses?" and he reached out and caught the Parson's sleeve. Now he, too, was stuck fast and it wasn't long before they were joined by a ploughman and a shepherd!

After a time they reached the city and there in the palace lived the King and his daughter. She had never been known to smile and the King had promised her hand in marriage to the first person who was able to make her laugh. Well, when the Princess saw the three girls, the Parson, the Bishop, the ploughman and the poor shepherd all falling over one another behind Dummling's golden Goose, she burst into peals of laughter.

The King came running and Dummling lost no time in asking permission to marry the Princess.

"Hmm," thought the King to himself. "I do not want this raggle taggle boy to marry my daughter. I must set him an impossible task to perform and when he fails, I will be able to refuse him."

And so the King told Dummling that before the marriage could take place he would first have to find a man who could drink a whole cellarful of wine.

Dummling scratched his head and then he remembered the old man in the forest. But when he returned to the glade the old man was not there. Instead, he found a short man with a miserable face.

"Oh, my, I am so terribly thirsty," he moaned. "I have already drunk a barrel of wine but I feel as if I could drain a lake dry!"

"You are just the man I am looking for!" cried Dummling and he led the man to the King's cellar.

The fat man rubbed his hands with glee.

"This is a sight for sore eyes!" the short man declared and soon he had emptied every bottle, keg, cask and barrel. The King was more vexed than ever. He decided to set another task and this time made it even harder.

"Find me a man who can eat a whole mountain of bread," he ordered, well satisfied that this would indeed prove impossible.

But Dummling went straight to the forest and there discovered a tall, thin man sitting on a log.

"I have just had four ovenfuls of bread for my supper but it has barely taken the edge of my appetite," he complained. Dummling pulled at his sleeve.

"I know a place where you can eat your fill," he said.

When he arrived back at the Palace the cooks set to work and kneaded their dough for a day and a night. When the bread was piled high it filled the whole courtyard!

The tall, thin man ate and ate and ate and within hours the mountain had become a molehill, and soon there was nothing left at all.

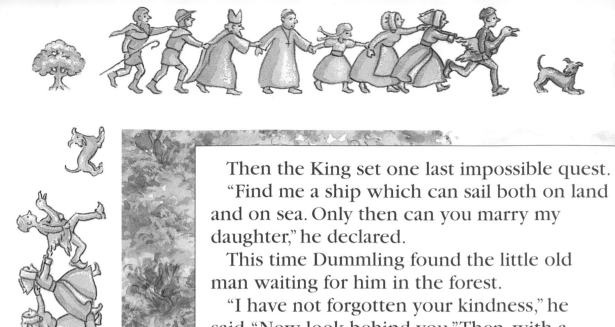

Then the King set one last impossible quest.

"Find me a ship which can sail both on land and on sea. Only then can you marry my daughter," he declared.

This time Dummling found the little old man waiting for him in the forest.

"I have not forgotten your kindness," he said. "Now look behind you." Then, with a great rustling of canvas, the most magnificent ship sailed into the glade.

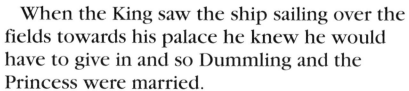

When the King saw the ship sailing over the fields towards his palace he knew he would have to give in and so Dummling and the Princess were married.